FOR AMY

Don't miss looking for Gustav on the endpapers!

All rights reserved. Published in the United States by Random House Studio,
an imprint of Random House Children's Books,
a division of Penguin Random House LLC, New York.

Random House Studio with colophon is a trademark of Penguin Random House LLC.

Visit us on the Web! rhcbooks.com

Educators and librarians, for a variety of teaching tools, visit us at RHTeachersLibrarians.com

Library of Congress Cataloging-in-Publication Data is available upon request.
ISBN 978-0-593-48747-1 (trade) — ISBN 978-0-593-48748-8 (lib. bdg.) — ISBN 978-0-593-48749-5 (ebook)

The artwork is drawn in ink and colored in Photoshop.
The text of this book is set in 17-point Eames Century Modern.
Interior design by Rachael Cole

MANUFACTURED IN CHINA
10 9 8 7 6 5 4 3 2 1
First Edition

GUSTAV IS MISSING!

A Tale of Friendship and Bravery

ANDREA ZUILL

RANDOM HOUSE STUDIO ⌂ NEW YORK

Little Cap lived with his best friend, Gustav, in their cozy house.

Little Cap needed a safe place because, in his opinion, the world held too many surprises . . .

and was filled with highly suspect individuals.

Frankly, the outside world was chaos.

It was nice having a home where Little Cap felt protected.

But even in your favorite places, bad things can happen.

Like when your best friend goes missing!

Oh no!
What was he going to do?

CHAOS!

POOR GUSTAV!

SURPRISES!

THE WORLD IS SCARY!

SUSPECT INDIVIDUALS!

FEAR!

With great determination, Little Cap pushed his fears out of his mind and got really serious.

He knew what he had to do.

He was going to find Gustav!

After packing some supplies, Little Cap headed
out into the great big world in search of his friend.

It wasn't long before he spotted some of his neighbors.
Being shy, Little Cap dreaded asking them if they'd
seen his friend. But he did it for Gustav!

It turned out they were pretty nice. Unfortunately, they couldn't help.

As he continued, Little Cap found that not everyone was easy to talk to. Some didn't want to be bothered.

Others seemed a little confused.

It was exciting when Little Cap found someone who *had* seen Gustav.

Soon Little Cap picked up his friend's trail.

And as he searched, Little Cap's mind began to wander and worry. Could Gustav be hurt? Maybe he was cold and wet?

What if, right
this minute, a
vicious beast was
threatening him?!

Little Cap walked a bit faster.

He was farther away from
home than he'd ever been.

The territory was rough,
and Little Cap's confidence
was being tested.

He nearly backed out of
crossing a deep canyon.

He almost rejected the idea
of scaling a sheer cliff.

YUCK!

And then something
unfortunate happened . . .
he stepped in something
really, really gross.

Even with the hardships, Little Cap's searching skills had improved.

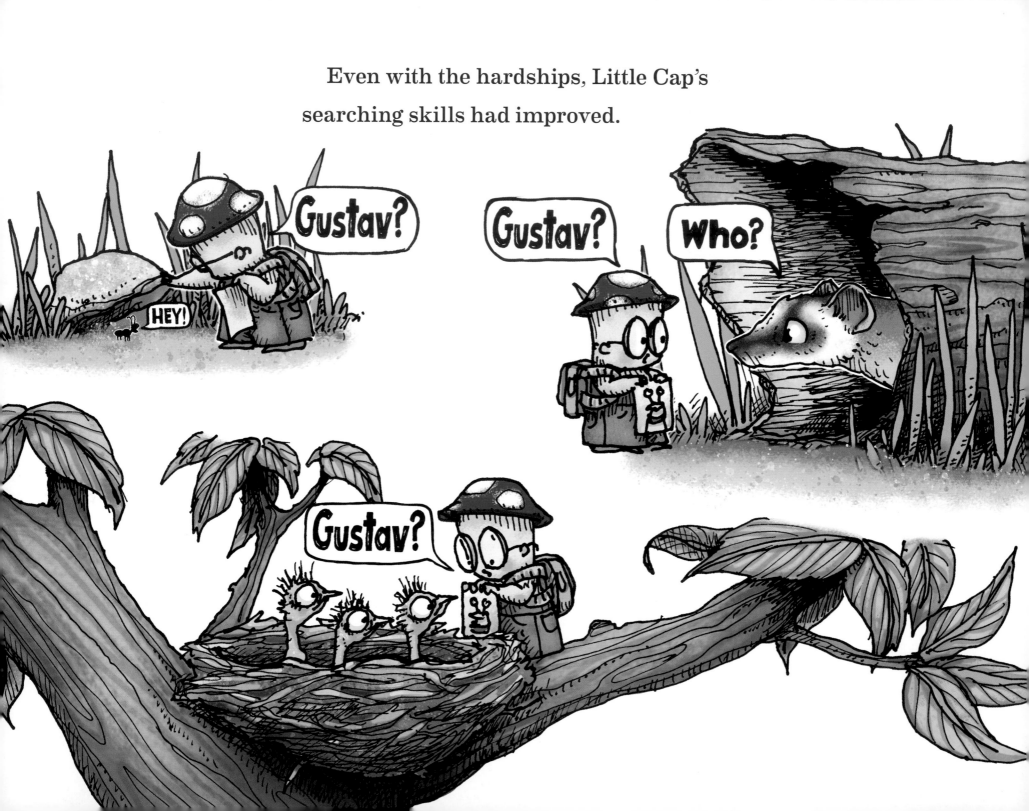

But there was still no Gustav. Little Cap was getting tired and fed up. Not only had he not found Gustav, but he hadn't even seen a single slug!

On the trip back home, Little Cap was feeling brave.

Still, it was a relief when they finally arrived home.

Little Cap and Gustav went
back to their safe, cozy lives.

But Little Cap had changed.

He loved telling friends all about his past adventures.

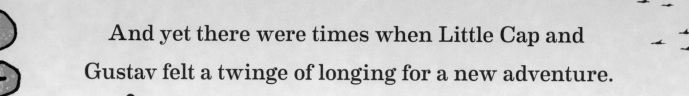

And yet there were times when Little Cap and
Gustav felt a twinge of longing for a new adventure.